The City of All-Worlds

Michael Jasper

UNWRECKED PRESS

The City of All-Worlds

Cover image by Enrique | Pexels

ISBN: 978-0692637036

Published by UnWrecked Press

Also by Michael Jasper

The City of All-Worlds

The humid night air crept closer, dripping onto the boy like tar as he slipped into his teacher's cave. Young Palapeeter walked on tiptoes, with a silver whistle in his right hand and a tarnished silver bell—its clapper pinched with a thumb and forefinger—in his left. In the cave where his master slept, there would be no excuse for noise.

Silence was needed, for Bartolamus the Sorcerer was dying.

The old man lay in a makeshift bed at the far end of the long, narrow cave he called home, covered in heavy blankets. As usual, though he was flat on his back with his eyes closed and his breathing shallow and rare, the old man held a pen of constant ink in his left hand, scribbling equations onto a worn scroll. Even at rest, Bartolamus was still working.

Running the length of the cave, illuminated by the flickering light of the globes pressed into the rock walls, stood bookcase after bookcase jammed full of books and papers of all sizes, colors, and shapes. On top of each bookcase, wedged into the few open spaces between books, sat miniature towers, keeps, and bridges, ancient structures untouched by rust.

"Master," Peet whispered, trembling.

One of Bartolamus' bright green eyes opened, though the pen never stopped scribbling.

"Master. I found your bell and whistle. I beg forgiveness for waking you, but you did say it was important—"

Peet's words failed him when, for the first time since his father had brought the boy to Bartolamus' cave from their family home at the edge of the Bluetip Mountains, his master put down his pen. Even when Bartolamus ate—even when the man used the chamber pot!—he never stopped scribbling out his theories.

"Boy," Bartolamus said softly, clearly. "Come closer."

"M-Master," Peet began. Surely his master didn't expect him to sit *next* to him? "I don't..."

"You will want to sit, my boy," Bartolamus said with a strange coughing sound. The old man was *laughing.*

"Good," Bartolamus said. "Now, I know you want to know about that whistle and that bell in your possession. That, my boy, is a long, long story."

Peet sat on the edge of his Master's bed and wished he hadn't spent the last two days—without sleep—crisscrossing the dusty streets of Southfort, searching for the old woman who sold him the whistle and the young girl who had bartered for Peet's lunch and his best pair of socks in exchange for the battered metal bell. Under Bartolamus' orders, he hadn't dared blow into the whistle or allowed the bell to ring.

"Don't worry," Bartolamus said as if reading his apprentice's mind. "I think my tale will keep your head from nodding."

"Yes, Mas—"

"Hush, now, boy, and *listen.*" Bartolamus picked up his pen again. "Since the start of recorded history..."

Since the start of recorded history, the City of All-Worlds has been the proud owner of a Portal.

Only a handful understood its workings, of course, but I've been a student of it all my life. This doorway onto other worlds was used to enrich the world of Subaridon with knowledge—as well as visitors—from other worlds. Commerce flowed into and out of the City, originating at the Portal, populating the paved streets with beauty and crime, danger and wonder, steel and flowers.

The Closure put an end to all of that.

The Closure of the City of All-Worlds began in a tavern, of all places, on the night before I was to begin my career.

From the moment my mentor had released me from my apprenticeship, I began drowning myself, one swallow at a time, in the Horse's Mouth Tavern. I did not want to work. Not even for the Royal Builders, the sole architects of the City. I yearned to do something more, something related to the Portal, though I was too young and foolish to know what I really wanted.

And so, I was in the process of getting properly drunk for the first time, when a petite woman in a purple cloak came over and stared down at me with a smirk on her blue-tinted face.

"A bit young," she said, crimson lips twitching into a smile, "to be this deep in your drink already, aren't you?"

I sat up and felt the world tilt. "Who's young?" I said, made bold by my drink. "What is age?"

The woman looked at the four empty mugs scattered around me like crooked towers and the half-full mug glued to my hand. Against her purple cloak, her skin was so pale it was almost blue. With a shock of knowledge that I knew I did not hide on my face, I realized she was from the other side of the Portal.

"Why such bitterness, builder?"

I flinched at that label, and then looked down at the inkstains on my hand, the blueprints at my side, and the architect's tool clipped to my vest: a combination compass, pencil scraper, level, and tension gauge all rolled into one.

"Have a seat and I'll explain it all to you, miss..."

To my shock, the woman gave another twitching of her lips and sat across from me.

"I am called Caution," she said. "Someone around here has to have it."

"I see. I am Bartolamus," I added, trying not to remember that I had to be awake before dawn the next morning to start my new life as Lower Architect for the Royal Builders.

"You are bitter, Bartolamus," Caution said. She placed her short-fingered hands on the table in front of me, palms down.

Each finger carried a ring of a different metal, with a stone of different color. Her thumb was as thin as a finger. "Tell like to hear more," she added.

"Because, I am just a mouse. Let me explain," I added quickly. "In the ugly buildings of the Research Quarter, there are rooms of men and women from all worlds, studying rodents. My fool of a former master helped design one of the newer towers on the banks of the Whiting."

Caution glanced away, losing interest. I was babbling.

"In any case. In this building, these researchers look to mice to find intelligence and theorize about how humans learn. They set the mice in complicated labyrinths, with cheese as a reward at one end, and caustic substances applied to them for every wrong turn. Pain is a wonderful motivator for learning and avoiding mistakes. And so, we are just like mice."

I leaned back against the rough wood of the booth, immeasurably proud of my theory and myself. Caution pushed back her hood, and her dark hair fell from it like a living thing. As she lowered her arms, I could see the crisscrossing scars on the inside of her wrists and the green and blue tattoos on the palms of her hands.

She was one of the Killaster Witches. Her tattoos told me that, and her scars told me that she'd killed herself many times to rise to her current position of power.

And one of the men at the bar was watching us in the mirror behind the dusty bottles.

"Tell me," she said at last, as her pale face shifted, her high cheekbones melting into a rounder, less human face. "What would you *rather* do, Little Mouse, instead of playing at building ugly towers and keeps?"

Glancing around the tavern, my eyes meeting those of the rough-faced man in the bar mirror, I turned back to Caution.

"What do you care about my dreams," I whispered, and added with a mischievous malice, "otherworlder?"

"You are a bright one," the woman said, her voice deepening. "We could use someone like you."

Her eyes were now multi-irised and glittering. I knew if I looked at her hands, there would be two fewer fingers on each hand. I wondered where her rings had gone.

"We?" I said.

"Some call us witches," the creature who called herself Caution said, her lips barely moving. "But we are so much more than that. We have knowledge of the rules of time and space that your people won't grasp for centuries. But we cannot do anything in the City without attracting the wrong kind of attention. Surely you know of the growing hatred for otherworlders ever since the murders in the slums last month."

"What..." I began, my voice cracking. "What murders?"

Caution stared at me for a long second. "Oh hell. Have you been so busy licking your master's boots that you haven't heard?"

The man at the bar now turned all of his attention on us.

"You know nothing of the murders and the fires in the ghetto that you Cityfolk call Downwind?"

I shook my head, no longer thirsty for more ale.

"Fucking *hell*. They said things were bad in the City, but this? Total ignorance? Simmering fucking hell."

The man at the bar stood and walked over to our table while Caution was talking. Under his dark brown cloak, I could see a glint of the dark blue armor worn by the soldiers of the King, old Dunimic the Wise. He slid next to me and pushed me closer to the wall, lodging splinters into my bony butt in the process.

"*Language*," the man said, his breath reeking of harsh whiskey. "Not the kind of language a lady would be usin'."

Caution had reverted back to the pale beauty I'd seen when she first approached me.

"I never claimed be such a lady," Caution said. "Now could you please explain why you've interrupted my colleague and me?"

The soldier laughed. "I'm not takin' orders from witches."

Caution began to rise from the booth, but the soldier grabbed both her ring-laden hands in his gloved right hand, pinning me to the wall with his left.

His voice was a hiss. "Let's be talkin' first before you get to leavin'."

The soldier slowly let go of her hands with a scratching sound as his metal glove came into contact with some of Caution's glittering rings.

"Now start tellin' me. What need are you and your sister witches havin' for some foolish boy, here in my City?"

"I don't talk to hired muscle." Caution rubbed her tattooed hands together. "*Your* city."

From under his whiskers, the soldier smiled. "You'll be doin' some talkin' today. I can be makin' this worth your while, along with our builder's boy here." The soldier pulled out a pouch of coins from his cloak and at the same time plucked my money pouch from my belt. He tossed both onto the table.

"Now," he said. "Let's be getting' to some *talkin'*."

The soldier's name was Graythorn, but whether that was his first name or last, I never knew. He was a lieutenant in the King's Guard, men and women who were Subaridon natives only, known as the best fighters, in wartime or peacetime.

Before I could fully sober up and realize what I was getting myself into, Graythorn the soldier and Caution the otherworlder had hatched a plan to get Caution and her sisters into the King's Tower the next morning to meet with Dunimic.

According to their stories, two fortnights ago an entire block of ramshackle homes outside the City walls had been burned to the ground by youths from the City. Two otherworld laborers living three doors away, still adjusting to live on our world, had been coerced into accepting blame for it. The two mute laborers, travelers to Subaridon from their dying world, had been taken by the King's Guard. They were sentenced to death.

"The public decapitations will take place tomorrow after the noon bells," Caution finished, "unless something is done."

"What is bein' in this for *you*?" Graythorn said.

"For me? I want to save two innocent boys from the foolish laws of your City. I want to bring the guilty parties to justice. But most of all, I want the damned sons and daughters of your damned City to stop killing my neighbors and my people!"

"I'll be helpin' you," he said after a pause. "If you'll be havin' me. I can get you in to the king. But you'll have to be followin' my every order, and not be deviatin'. Clear?"

For the first time all night, he turned to me. "And you, boy? Are you bein' with us?"

I nodded, no longer trusting my own voice. I probably would have squeaked like one of the mice I spoke of earlier.

"Good," he growled. "Because I have a role I'll need you to play if we're to be getting' in to see his majesty tomorrow."

Hours later, I half-walked, half-staggered past the iron-gated towers of Forsooth, my path lit by bright green globes dangling from every doorway. Fifty-feet-tall fortresses of wood and metal, the dwellings of the academics lined the paved thoroughfare. The red-tiled roofs grew higher the closer I came to my home, two blocks from the outer wall and the razor-tipped Northeastern Gate, almost within sight of the slum on the other side of the City wall (if I cared to look in that direction, which I did not).

Back in my rooms, I was unable to sleep. Caution had pulled me close after Graythorn had left us, and she would not release me until I'd learned a dozen words of power from her world. I didn't dare speak them, so I covered my last blueprint from my pouch with phonetic breakdowns of her Killaster words.

"Use only if all is lost," she whispered, her strange, otherworldly eyes scanning the nearly-empty tavern around us.

"There is great power in them. Use them on *Graythorn* if you must. Now write them for me one more time, in your language."

Instead of sleeping, I walked through the well-furnished rooms of my quarters, passing the burnt orange leather chairs of my parlor and stopping in front of my collection of miniature towers and intricately-designed buildings in my study. These carefully-molded, fully-functional automatons and accurate recreations were my pride and joy.

I looked at my idealized Cityscape in front of me. *This* was how a City should be designed: towers mixed in with low buildings, evenly-spaced water towers, wide streets and sidewalks, mechanical carriages inside every dwelling. I wanted to combine all the technology of our world with the insights of the countless other worlds we made contact with through the Portal. Perfection and harmony.

Suddenly, I had an urge to run my hand across the smooth oaken tabletop and destroy my perfect City, embarrassed of my childish dreams. For there were injustices being carried out on the streets of the City outside my windows, in the shantytowns outside the City walls.

And I'd been sheltered from them my entire life, until today. Too tired to do anything more, I spared my miniature Cityscape and slept like the dead.

I woke to the sight of Graythorn standing over my bed, and his presence encouraged me to dress and follow him down the steps in under a minute. Outside, the sun had not yet risen, but the foot traffic was already building as we approached the river and the King's Tower in the middle of it.

Graythorn and I walked the wide black stretch of the Paveway, the smooth road already growing warm under our boots. We walked in silence to the raised drawbridge in front of the wide island where the Zither and Whiting met.

Even though I'd lived my entire life in the City, the King's Tower always took my breath away. A series of turrets made up the lowest layer, running the entire circumference of the castle. Some of the square windows inside the turrets were already lit up, and figures and shadows passed through their interiors as the various workers started their day. I could see one old woman bent over a desk in a tiny turreted room, while a wild-haired young man did jumping jacks in another.

Behind and above the lower layer of turrets were the walkways. Connecting the top room of each turret with the main turret that comprised the actual King's Tower itself, the white metal walkways stretched like thick strands of spider webs. Dark-robed figures passed from the turrets onto the walkways in silence, disappearing into the smooth stone of the King's Tower.

"Ready, boy?" Graythorn said, watching me.

As I was gazing at the Tower, the drawbridge had lowered silently. We followed the dozen other travelers across the wide metal and wood of the drawbridge, which had dropped down and unfolded itself across the river while I was gaping upwards.

"When should I begin my speaking in tongues?" I said to him, my voice a whisper. The plan had been for me to act insane, assuring us the head of the King's receiving line.

"Not now," the soldier hissed. He pushed me through a heavy door almost indistinguishable from the smooth stone walls. The air in this octagonal room was thick and warm.

"There's been a changin' of plans," Graythorn said.

Next to me was a fireplace that covered the northern wall, stoked high with orange flames. A series of vents had been built into the ceiling, sucking the fire's heat up and into the rest of the castle.

"You are no longer bein' touched in the head as we were agreein' yesterday. You are now bein' one of the few survivors from that damnable fire in Downwind two fortnights ago. You'll be claimin' that the fires started in your shack, and the two otherworlders were bein' nowhere in sight."

I didn't have time to scream before Graythorn threw me into the fire.

The right half of my face took the brunt of the fire. Most of my outer cloak was instantly burned away, allowing me to get free of the flames with only slight burns on my back. But I could feel the searing hot welts on my face, already blistering. I fell to the stone floor, rolling out flames and moaning.

"There," Graythorn said from above me. "Now you are makin' a fine victim for us. We got to be convincin' to see the King."

On all fours, I tried to slip past him and make for the door, but he clipped me upside the head and pulled me to my feet.

"Easy," the soldier said, throwing a small handful of reddish dust onto my burns. Some of the searing heat receded.

Graythorn led me through the curving corridors into the main tower. According to the soldier's reasoning, a survivor of one of the worst fires in the City's slums wouldn't be coming to see the King with his clothing perfect and without burns.

"Time bein' short and all," Graythorn said. "We had to improvise. Be glad I was findin' this pinch of dust for you."

"You could have at least told me," I said, holding one hand to my cheek and wiping away tears of anger with the other.

"And have you disappearin' on us, or losin' courage at the final moment? Nah. This is bein' the best way."

Claiming in a loud voice that he had a Downwind victim with him, Graythorn was able to get us to the front of the line of people waiting to see the King. The King and his advisor only saw Cityfolk every third day, for an hour, so we had a brief window of time to convince him to remand the two death sentences. Caution and her sisters were nowhere to be found.

The first otherworlder we'd seen since entering the King's Tower stood guard in front of the double doors leading to the throne room. I forgot my pain when I looked up at him. He wore a bright silver metal suit that encased his entire body except for his hands, and a transparent shield covered his mottled black and brown face. Four of his eight eyes tracked Graythorn while the other four watched the crowd, ignoring me altogether.

An eel-like hand made up of suckers instead of fingers reached out in front of Graythorn. The creature in the metal armor clicked and grunted at us, his tone telling me that we were not to break in line as we'd been doing. After a short discussion with Graythorn in a foreign tongue, the big creature stepped back, letting us through the doors.

Inside the throne room, the king and his advisor sat at simple wooden chairs at the far end of a rectangular black table. Another otherworlder, also encased in silver body armor stood in the shadows of the room, next to a tapestry depicting a detailed, multi-colored map of Subaridon. The rest of the room was open to the sunlight in floor-to-ceiling windows with the red and yellow drapes thrown wide to let in the morning sun.

The light dazzled me as I was pushed toward the black table. Sitting at the other end of the table, along with two women dressed exactly like her in shiny purple robes, Caution the witch.

"Is this the survivor, then?" The King's voice was deep and soft, full of guarded curiosity. I could see that he was not completely at ease with the three women at his table.

His advisor, a black-haired man wearing loose-fitting chain mail to hide his protuberant gut, looked from me to the three women at the other end of the table.

"Is this *him*?" he said, looking from Graythorn to Caution.

"Yes," Caution murmured, staring at my wounds and ragged clothing. "This is the boy. See how vicious his wounds are, my lord? This sort of violence cannot continue, as I and my sisters have been telling you all morning."

King Dunimic nodded slowly, his simple silver crown bobbing on his thinning hair. His beard was short, and his gray mustaches were carefully waxed, curling twice in upon itself. With his advisor leaning close, he never took his gaze from me.

"Your wounds," the king said. "They look fresh, my boy."

"Your majesty," Caution began, but Dunimic silenced her with a raised hand.

"My boy," he said to me. "How did you survive in the slum? Surely you lack the strength to live in such an environment, with your slender build. I can see inkstains on your hands, and softness in your cheek. Explain yourself, my boy."

My mind spun. I fought the urge to look to Graythorn for assistance. Instead I looked down at the table between the King and myself and tried to imagine what life would be like outside the City's walls. What was it like to live in a dwelling without a roof, to fight for my next meal with others, to live on the scraps of those inside the City? My mind recoiled.

I wanted to think I could survive out there, but the King's brief summation of me was apt. I was a city boy, soft and spoiled, without the slightest ability to fend for myself.

"Majesty," I said, my voice cracking. "I..."

Caution placed a cold hand on my arm, stopping me. She had dropped her disguise, and her blue face seethed with rage.

"No," she whispered, rising to her feet. "Say no more."

The King had already motioned to his guards, but he wasn't fast enough to stop Caution's sister witches from dropping onto the floor. The two creatures scurried across the room on all fours toward the sliding metal door that sealed off the Portal from the rest of the Tower.

As the first otherworld guard dove onto the two slithering witches, Graythorn pulled his sword and dagger, betrayal etched into his lined face. He launched his dagger at Caution the witch just as the second otherworld guardian from the door tackled him. Caution took the dagger in her belly, and bright bluish-red blood spilled out from under her fingers.

I dropped under the table, where I could see the King's boots as he pushed away from the table, the iron scabbard of his sword quivering as he pulled his sword. On my left, her blood now staining the floor, I could see Caution's three-fingered hands pull the dagger from her belly, and then she leaped onto the table.

Two footsteps sounded on the table, heading for the King. I realized nearly too late what she was doing. I tried to make Caution's words of power from last night come to my throat, but my brain was stalled. My fool's tongue was stuck with shock.

All I could do was hoist the end of the massive table with all my might, hoping to knock her off balance. I was rewarded with a thudding sound as she fell to the floor. After dropping the table end, I risked a look over at the King.

He still stood, looking at me with a quizzical expression, as if wondering where I came from. Graythorn's dagger was lodged in his chest. The King's last action in this world was a final swing of his sword, beheading Caution, the otherworld witch on the floor next to him.

The witch's sisters screamed in unison even as the armored guardian encased them in a bristling field of energy, rendering them immobile. Graythorn evaded the other guardian just as the King's advisor aimed a long black weapon at Graythorn.

Graythorn's face dropped when he saw his own dagger imbedded in his King's chest, and that was when I turned to run.

The other guardian was moving toward me even as I sprinted for the windows at the far end of the hall. The eight-eyed creature would have surely killed me had Graythorn not slid a chair into the guardian's path, slowing the creature. And then the advisor's weapon exploded, and Graythorn toppled backwards.

Ripping down one of the heavy curtains as I ran, I spun myself inside of it, closed my eyes, and shrieked. I fell.

As I was fleeing to the sound of screaming klaxons from the top of the King's Tower, I realized that I had remembered at least one word of power taught to me by the traitorous Caution. I had screamed it at the window just before I hit it, and the force of the word had shattered the glass before I slammed into it. I glanced back and up and saw that most of the foundation around the window had been blown away as well.

Limping toward the drawbridge, I vowed to avenge the deaths in the throne room, all but those of Caution and her sisters. The witches could burn forever, for all I cared, even as all twelve of Caution's words of power burned now, inside my mind.

* * * * *

All around me, voices were screaming out the King's name, while in the same breath cursing otherworlders for his death. The news had spread quickly of how the King had been stabbed right in his own throne room, and how otherworld witches had conspired to the act with a traitorous soldier. There were also murmurings of a young boy from Downwind who used his burned face as a ticket into the throne room.

I covered my face with my hood and nearly ran down the wide lanes of the King's Paveway.

I made it to within a hundred paces of the outer gates when I remembered my rooms in Forsooth. In my rooms were all my worldly belongings, but most of all, they contained my idealized Cityscape. I stopped dead in the middle of the road, with soldiers on horseback pounding past me toward the Tower, where the klaxons continued to wail.

No, I told myself. I must flee. Now.

But before I could stop myself, I stepped off the Paveway and disappeared into the maze of side streets and alleyways that connected the storefronts and hotels and taverns along the main road. I ran east and then north, pushing myself hard until I hit the Zither River. I ran into the river without hesitation.

The water was breath-stoppingly frigid, and the current nearly carried me to the iron bars in the outer wall, straining the river and leading outside. I made it to the other bank, crawling on hands on knees, and ran past the outlying houses and factory buildings of the Miller's Quarter. The air grew thick with the smoke and stink of the grain and milling factories. At least the smoke would hide me from the guards who were surely coming for me.

Panting and almost screaming with each exhalation, I made it to the rear of my building. The apartments were quiet, and all the shades had been drawn against the eastern sun. The silence threatened to unnerve me.

The door to my rooms was still locked, but that meant nothing to me. Anyone could have slipped inside and turned the deadbolt again. I turned the key and stepped inside. In my bedroom and began grabbing the oldest of my City towers. I grabbed an old coat, tied the sleeves together, and threw all three dozen pieces of the City into the coat. Jingling and rattling, I passed up the temptation to grab food or more clothes. I would get by on the outside, somehow.

"Not what I would've chosen to take with me," a raspy female voice said, nearly stopping my heart.

The person who spoke stood on my couch, where I'd spent many late nights with my blueprints and drawings spread out in front of me. She was short and stout, like an overgrown young girl.

"How did you get in here?" I hissed, still out of breath.

"Think you live in some kind of fortress?" the woman said, hopping down off the couch. The floor trembled with the impact as her bulky boots hit the ground. "Slipped in while you were off with your new friend."

"Graythorn?" I said. "You knew him?" I looked at the door, thinking I heard heavy footsteps approaching.

"That the name he used?" The woman laughed. "Guess it fits him. Time to get out of here. Now." Her tone of voice, not to mention her double-bladed axe, stifled any argument from me.

On my way out the door, I passed the strange woman. Her face was smooth as a polished white stone, just the hint of pink to it in her cheeks. Instead of going down to the entrance, she pushed me up the stairs, toward the roof. I didn't dare resist.

"Surely you've flown before?" the woman asked.

I looked at the small woman next to me and began to laugh. Below us, I could see members of the King's Guard massing. My laughter dying on my lips, I looked at the winged contraption waiting on the roof. Four long, curving wings reached almost to the ground, each wing comprised of what had to be three dozen pieces of thin metal. Each piece connected to the next piece like a joint, making the wing bend like a gigantic arm.

I'd heard stories about such flying crafts, many made in the Reaching Swamp and tested in suicidal leaps from the Bluetip Mountains next to the swamplands. I'd never seen one up close.

"You weren't joking," I said.

"I don't joke," she said, moving toward the craft. She held out a stubby hand to me. "Maudra," she said, squeezing my hand in hers. "From the Reaching Swamp. You are?"

"I am Bartolamus," I said, almost groaning from her grip.

She let go at last, just as the wind began to pick up and footsteps pounded up the steps behind us. Maudra lifted a hatch, and I climbed inside the cold metal box, smelling something bittersweet, and she ran around to the front and climbed in.

Through an opening in my box I watched her grab two handles on either side of her and begin to spin them. Sparks flew and the corded muscles in her arms bulged, and a wild clattering noise started up.

A heartbeat later, with Maudra churning the handles, we lifted into the air.

I pushed my coat out of the way so I could see better, and that was when I realized I was not alone in the back of the flying machine. Two red-skinned otherworlders lay folded into the corners of the box, wrapped in blankets. Silent, with their eyes closed tight, they seemed to take no notice of me. I could barely tell where the first hairless, four-armed creature stopped and the second one began. With a shudder I risked a look through the hatch. Three of the King's archers were taking aim at us from fifty feet below.

"Maudra..." I tried to say, but my voice was gone.

The flying machine gave a sudden lurch and lifted higher into the sky. Before I closed the hatch again, I was given a truly magnificent view of the City of All-Worlds from above. It would be me last look at it, though I didn't know it then.

The City opened up below us like the tapestry hanging in the King's throne room. Behind us, to the southwest, stood the turrets of the King's Tower, the Tower itself enfolded in a protective cloud that had most likely been thrown there by the mages in the outer turrets as a safety measure. The Whiting and the Zither came together around the tower, rivers that were much wider from the air, one slightly green in color, the other lighter and less muddy. The black Paveway unfurled in front of the King's Tower like a black tongue, and church steeples poked into the sky like accusing fingers. Framing the entire scene was the razor-tipped wall, protecting the City from the slums and the world outside.

We flew less than ten feet above the wall, and then I saw the lush green grass and the first evergreen trees of the King's Forest. A hundred feet below us, but growing closer as the flapping wings of our craft slowed, was a farming village with crisscrossing dirt paths and smoky fires and chimney smoke reaching up into the air to greet us.

A small boy looked up, one of the few villagers whose head had not yet been bowed down by their labors and work. His mouth formed a perfect circle of shock as he gaped at us.

Wracked with sudden guilt over the events of that morning, I didn't dare look at my fellow passengers in their grim silence. The King was dead, and nothing would ever be the same.

Once we touched down in a field on the other side of the Forest. Maudra was covered in sweat, and her face was flushed almost purple. I helped Maudra from the craft, and then we both fell to the soft, forgiving grasslands outside the City of All-Worlds. The two otherworlders remained inside the craft.

I slept for an exhausted hour on the ground, on the wrong side of the City walls.

O utside the City was a land I'd never known existed. Coming to my senses sooner than Maudra, I pulled myself to my feet and crept over to the flying craft, hoping I would not wake Maudra and have to confront her and what she knew. The four wings of the craft drooped low as if they were as exhausted as its pilot and engineer. I peeked inside the hatch, afraid I'd see the red, expressionless faces of the two otherworlders again, but the two creatures were gone. Breathing more easily, I reached into the craft and eased out my coat full of my City buildings.

My eyes burned with guilt and shame as I looked at the slightly battered buildings clumped together inside my coat. I was the one who allowed the witches entry into the King's throne room, and I survived only because of Graythorn's sacrifice. I again felt the urge to destroy the pieces of my Cityscape, the last remaining evidence of my childhood. And my innocence.

Maudra came awake a moment later.

"Help me with my wingcraft," she said.

We pushed the surprisingly light vehicle into the cover of the trees and covered it with fallen branches as best we could. Maudra pushed away from her aircraft with a sigh.

"What of the two otherworlders?" I asked. "Where are they?"

Maudra shrugged. "They are free to move about the world as they please now. They're free. Just like you."

I stared at her for a long moment. Something good had come of my actions today, I decided. It wasn't much relief, but I had to take it where I found it.

"Come," she said. "I want to be at Andros' before nightfall."

Maudra began walking south, towards the City. I had to jog to catch up to her—despite the shortness of her legs, the woman kept a harsh pace. With the sun turning red low in the sky to the east of us, warming my unburned left cheek, we passed the village on a dirt path.

Neither of us spoke until we were well beyond the outlying village. With the City wall growing taller in front of us, I could not keep my silence any longer.

"Why?" was all I could manage.

Maudra leaped over a wide stream that I blundered into, splashing like a dog. Maudra gave me an angry look.

"City boy," she said, clucking her tongue at me. "Noisy."

We walked another minute before she looked at me again. "Why do I help you, is that what you are asking?"

I nodded, my heartbeat skipping with the way she looked at me, part anger and part pity.

"There's code among soldiers, boy," she began. "We view all other soldiers as pieces of ourselves. Together we form a whole. If a piece of us is corrupt, we must help that piece of the whole." Maudra paused and adjusted the axe strapped to her back. "The man you called Graythorn was a friend, and he was a fellow soldier. I'm simply righting his wrong. Understand me, boy?"

"I'm Bartolamus," I said. Hands on my knees, I sucked in air. "Not 'boy,' Miss Maudra."

Maudra laughed softly and nodded. She turned and began walking again, still laughing under her breath.

We arrived back outside the City gates just as night fell. My coat protected me from the growing cold—winter was only a month off—but the towers and miniature mechanisms in the coat pockets weighed me down, adding twenty pounds to my already fatigued back. If we had gone much further, I don't doubt that she would have thrown me over her shoulder and kept on walking. And then we were there.

"Welcome to Riverrun Alley." Maudra nodded at a ramshackle building on the other side of a river that I recognized as the Zither. The building was lit with a rainbow of shimmering colors. "Andros'," Maudra said, as if that was all I needed to know. "Come."

All my life I'd heard horror stories about the people and creatures living in the slums. "Those slum people did this" or "That happened late last night in the Alley." Other stories told of how the slum dwellers would waste their days, out of their mind on cheap drink or illegal herbs brought up from the Kazzikian Forest or in the Reaching Swamp. And most of all, stories were told of the crime in the Alley: the night thieves who would steal from the poor, or the eye-for-an-eye justice that allowed murder and other violences without question.

All of that stood in front of me once I stepped off the rope bridge that crossed the Zither River. Though the crooked streets stretching out in front of me were dark, I could see that the Alley was more than just a collection of shacks thrown up against one another. Dirt paths wound around leaning buildings held together by questionable means, opening into a circular square where a fire burned in a rusted barrel.

Hooded figures were gathered around the barrel, though most were walking toward the colorfully-lit building I'd seen from the other side of the river. Andros' Bar.

"Come," Maudra said. "I'll buy you dinner. Then you're on your own, boy." She touched my shoulder and got me moving toward the tavern. "Sorry. Bartolamus."

With the last of the redness disappearing from the sky, I felt suddenly vulnerable in front of Andros'. My apprehension grew as I saw more clearly who—or what—was standing around the fire barrel. Their cloaks could not hide their otherworldly forms. Two were multi-armed Walkers from Assurinto, if I remembered correctly, and one was a wide eight-eyed creature of the same race as the King's guardians in his throne room. The others I could not recognize.

Inside Andros', I felt warm for the first time all day. The colored lights I'd seen from outside were actually mismatched phosphor lights painted over in various hues. The place was comfortably crowded, filled with beings of all sizes and shapes. I saw humans of all colors drinking and eating with otherworlders of all races. I kept trying to find the two otherworlders who had ridden over the wall with us, but there must have been long gone, either back to Downwind or to the distant Fort cities.

Reaching the bar, I felt onto a stool next to Maudra.

"Don't get too comfortable," Maudra said, rapping on the smooth black wood of the bar. "Unless you plan on drinking Andros' firewater all night. Bar's for the serious drinker."

"Hey hey!" a high-pitched voice shouted from somewhere behind the bar. "About time you came back to visit, Maudra!"

"Been too long, I know," Maudra said, looking into the windows on the other side of the bar. "We're here for your best meal, Andros. Hope you got some good rat stew back there."

As Maudra and the high-pitched voice bantered back and forth, a shiver passed through me. I saw the reflection of what had to be the bar's owner in the black glass. A blue-black shadow outlined in glinting white light, Andros the Wight was standing directly in front of me. He disappeared the second my eyes left the reflective glass.

"So this is the boy who visited the King this morning, eh?"

I squinted into the air in front of me from where the question had come, but saw nothing but a reflected, rippling shadow in the glass. My eyes began to ache from looking into the glass and back to the air in front of me. It felt like trying to live in two different worlds at once

"Maudra," the high voice said in a mock scolding tone. "Why didn't you tell me it was his first visit here?" The air in front of me began to ripple like a mirage over the hot Paveway. "I could've at least stepped out of my stealth mode."

When the rippling stopped, a pale, barrel-shaped man stood in front of me. His face was hairless, not even eyelashes or brows to protect his dark eyes.

"I am Andros," the man said, winking. "Welcome to my bar."

"We need dinner, Andros," Maudra said, watching me.

"I have just the thing." The bald man snapped his fingers and disappeared again. "Be right back."

"Why does he do that?" I asked Maudra.

"It's his natural state. He's an otherworlder, too, you know. From a world of shadow people." Her thick legs dangled two feet above the warped wooden floor. She had taken off her leg armor, and the skin of her legs was bright and smooth.

"Take a look around you, Bartolamus," Maudra continued. "This is nothing like the City, where otherworlders try so hard to fit in and match the majority humans."

As a bottle of bright white wine appeared on the bar behind us, followed by two opaque glasses, I gazed at the denizens filling the tavern. Sitting at the bar to my immediate left sat a white-robed Mendicant from the Exile's Tundra far to the north, his forehead scar blazing red with reflected light. He glanced at me and frowned, then went back to his heated discussion about the benefits of null-gravity travel to the dog-faced Polanch licking a tar-like substance from his hairy paw. Six gigantic men in leather vests sat at a tiny table covered in bottles and plates stacked high, the furry skin of each man a different shade of brown, apparently depending on the number of empty bottles in front of them. They could have passed for human had it not been for their oversized, four-nostriled noses and fur covering every exposed inch of their muscle-bound bodies.

"Hagurupk fighters," Maudra said in soft voice.

More strange, otherworldly creatures surrounded us, and I nearly fell off my stool looking at all of them. I suddenly felt very, very thirsty.

"Easy, there," Maudra said, placing her hand on mine before I could take another drink. "Don't be drinkin' it like water. Plus I don't care to see a boy get shitty on me."

She turned me around in my chair as two bowls of steaming food were set in front of us.

I swallowed hard. "Ah, this isn't rat stew, is it?"

Maudra laughed and dabbed at her lips with a napkin, a strangely delicate movement. "I thought about it. But didn't want you havin' a bad aftertaste tonight after you leave here."

I swallowed a hot mouthful of carrots, starch plants, gravy, and bluebeans. All delicious. I forced myself to eat slower as Maudra's words sank in. After this, I was alone. I drank more wine and tried not to think about tomorrow.

After the meal, the wine filling my head with sand, I rested my elbows on the bar and listened. At some point Maudra slipped away, but caught up with my wine and the talk of the tavern, I never heard her leave.

Andros shook me awake later with an unseen hand. He led me to the door as the lights began winking out. The other customers had left.

"She left this for you," Andros said, fading in and out of my vision. He handed me a tiny four-winged mechanism, a perfect replica of her flying machine. I tucked the flying machine deep into a secret pocket in a cuff of my pants, down low.

"You learn fast. Now stay safe," Andros said, and then he pushed me out the door.

Outside I was confronted with a vast blackness. Even at night, the City was always lit up, glowing green lights stuck twenty feet up on every building, or smoking lamps hanging in doorways that succeeded in pushing away the dark. Here in the Alley, the roads and shacks I knew were ahead of me were invisible.

The late-summer air was still warm, but a cold breeze from the north caught me as I inched my way down the front steps of the tavern. I could smell the stale smell of the Zither passing next to me, carrying with it the city's pollutants and garbage.

All sense of wonder at the Alley's grimy, alien beauty fled when the wind was blocked by uncountable large bodies. From their harsh breathing, along with the smell of leather, I was pretty sure I was surrounded by most, if not all, of the Hagurupk fighters from the bar.

Before I could speak I was picked up and spun around. Rough hands pulled at my clothes, pulling off my coat and reaching into my pockets. My towers and buildings and replicas, the only reason I'd returned to the City, were being taken from me.

I went berserk then, screaming and biting and clawing. I kicked out and was rewarded by a low moan, and then one of the warriors threw me. They were gone by the time I landed, along with all my worldly possessions except for the clothes on my back and one broken tower made of metal and wood. I touched the cuff of my ripped pants, and was rewarded with the feel of the cold metal lump of Maudra's gift, her miniature flying machine.

Welcome to Riverrun Alley, I imagined her saying to me with a cool smile. *Your new home.*

I woke the next morning with a hacking cough and a handful of dead skin from my burned cheek in my lap. I'd spent most of the night working the tiny mechanisms of Maudra's gift, learning how the wings raised and lowers through pulleys and winches. At some point I must have dozed off.

When I woke, I decided I'd better get to know my new city.

I walked all morning, learning more with each step. While the City was centered on the King's Tower and the outstretched branches of the Paveway coming out from it, the Alley was organized by the boundaries of the Zither to the north and the City wall to the west. All the rest was barely contained chaos.

This lack of formal structure fascinated me. The Alley was not restrained by any law or rules. It simply existed, scrabbling through each day as best it could. It was not built so much as un-built.

Within half an hour I came across the food center of the Alley. The youngest and oldest sellers sat on the outskirts, hawking their misshapen black potatoes and shrunken ears of wormy redcorn. They bragged about the quality of their vegetables and fruits in spite of the smell of rot in the air. A muscle-bound butcher waved flies off the hanging sausages from his multi-leveled cart, and ensured me that his spiny rockular was pulled fresh from the Azure Sea that morning. How the man had brought the rank green fish the many leagues from the sea was a question I didn't stop long enough to ask him.

As I was walking through the food market, I saw one of the thugs who robbed me the night before. Before I could stop myself, I hurried past the western edge of the food bazaar, following the wide, muscular creature in faded brown leather.

As I followed the oversized fighter, thinking of the tiny mechanisms the buildings from my Cityscape, a formula began to take shape in my mind. It was similar to the blueprints from my apprenticeship with the Royal Builders, but in this case, the purpose was not to build up, but to destroy. I thought about the energy held in created objects, such as Maudra's flying machine, and the sciences I had learned about with the Royal Builders. Surely if I undid the bindings holding an object something together, great energy would be released.

As I walked, I took out Maudra's flying machine once again. As I touched the workings of it, unraveling a wing here, loosening a pin there, my mind opened up, and the words of power taught to me by Caution the witch filled my mind.

Hurrying through the broken ruins of the Old Walls, approaching the southern corner of the City walls, I felt something change in the air. I had completed the calculations of what I now thought of as my "un-building formula," and the half-assemble machine in my hands was growing hot to the touch.

"Thief!" I cried out. The Hagurupk stopped and spun faster than I could follow. He flashed a wicked grin; he recognized me.

When I was two paces away the thief, who was drawing a scimitar from his holster, I launched the pieces of the flying machine at him. Before it struck him, I screamed the words of Killaster that I'd learned late last night, three sharp, burning words that ripped at my vocal cords.

The energy of the words was focused through the unbuilt flying machine, turning it into a glowing projectile. I was rewarded with a bring green burst of energy as the ball of unbuilt materials hit the fighter in the belly. The fighter's blade, hat, rings, and boots went flying. He landed on his back, and one of the towers from my Cityscape rolled free of his hand.

When I picked up the tower, I realized what I'd just done. I sat down hard in the dirt, looking from my tower to the Hagarupk's boots and rings splayed out around me, wondering at what I'd created. Or un-created, in this case.

This was going to require further research, I decided.

But as soon as I turned away from his unconscious body, I heard a series of sounds that haunt me to this day. The earth shook with a clap of thunder and the screech of metal. A horn blew for almost ten heartbeats, followed by what sounded like hundreds of angry voices rushed towards me from the west.

From the hard ground I lifted my head, and I saw them. The first wave of the people who had been forced from the city by the new King. Some humans but most of them otherworlders, they trudged slowly away from the City, carrying all their belongings in their arms and on their bent backs. Looking lost and angry, there must have been hundreds of them. And they were headed straight for us.

Hard on the heels of the Closure of the City of All-Worlds and the discovery of my new sorcery of un-building, the Lowlies arrived.

Turning my back on the Hagurupk thief, I counted close to two-dozen different otherworlder species wandering shellshocked through the Alley that day. I saw a family of Kanilaro, humanoid creatures from a world similar to ours, but with less sunlight. Their swathed faces and bodies could have hidden any creature, but I knew they were the Kanilaro for their keening song and their beaklike noses that poked out of their bandages like accusing fingers. The largest of the Kanilaro carried two children on his back, his bass voice singing what sounded like a soothing melody to his whimpering young ones.

By the time more Kanilaro had passed, along with clumps of Brecken, families of horse-headed Vaganbus, and many more creatures I could not name, I was starting to feel overwhelmed.

This was *my* new home, I'd wanted to say. Not yours. How would they survive here in the Alley? Judging from the fancy clothes many of them still wore, and the unrealistic conglomeration of belongings they'd brought with them, the otherworlders were completely unprepared for life in the slums. Even I felt superior to the newest members of Riverrun Alley.

Many of the Lowlies, on their way past me, vowed revenge for their injustices. All of them cursed the new King's name and mourned the loss of Dunimic. Most believed this cleansing decree, ridding the city of all otherworlders, was only a temporary thing by the new king, Dunshinham, until his brother's murder was avenged and order restored.

But that has yet to happen. The City gates remain closed.

Years passed, and I spent my first decades of my new life in Riverrun Alley, working with my hands, studying my newfound sorcery, un-building those who committed acts of violence, making new friends, and encountering old friends again. I kept my ear always bent toward the City, eager for news about the Portal and the new King. I heard rumors of keys that would open the gates to the City, but they'd been hidden and lost for years.

And since that day, the City has been closed to me and so many of my friends. I ached to go back inside, so badly I had to move out of sight of the city. And I never forgot the words of power taught to me by Caution the witch, the words that I have taught my students, along with the sorcery of un-building. Yet I vowed, as long as there was breath in my body, to never stop trying to return and reopen the City of All-Worlds.

But now both my time and my breath have grown short.

A s dawn filled the cave with pinkish-orange light, Palapeeter the apprentice blinked for what felt like the first time in hours and realized his Master was no longer speaking.

Peet didn't dare move.

"Since that time, I've been haunted by both the death of King Dunimic as well as the closeness of the Portal. I knew Dunsinham was wasting the Portal's potential, and rumor had it he'd shut it down for good, closing off Subaridon from all other worlds. I couldn't remain in Riverrun Alley, so close to the City and the dead Portal. So I left my friends behind and headed south, through the Emptied Lands and into Southfort. I vowed to make amends with my research into my newfound sorcery."

The old man lifted a shaking hand and motioned to the objects in his apprentice's hands.

"Now, boy, I ask you to ring that bell and blow that whistle."

Peet did as he was told, and the night was filled with a whistling and a ringing that continued long after the boy had set down the two instruments. Bartolamus had set down his pen at last, and he stood, unwavering.

"My old friends have been awaiting my call. They will follow me north into the City again. We will find the All-Worlds Portal. For the jingling sounds you hear are indeed, the keys to the City of All-Worlds. For the last eight decades, I've not been idle. Along with my sorcery, I've been studying the workings of the gates to the City, and I think I have the means to un-build them and open the City once again."

Peet spun at the sound of the jangling keys coming from outside the cave mouth. He'd only half-believed in the keys up until that point. When the short, white-haired woman jogged into the cave, Peet knew that he had much to learn about the rest of the world. Or worlds.

"About time," the woman said, slightly out of breath. She unstrapped a wicked-looking axe from her back, glaring at Peet.

Bartolamus nodded at her with the hint of a smile. He continued in a soft voice. "With the keys that Miss Maudra has at last found, the City of All-Worlds will be free again. With the Portal operational again, the people of our world can start to grow again, sharing knowledge with those who live on the other side of our Portal. And I, at last, can die a happy man."

Something else entered the cave, two red figures that slipped free of the darkness outside to stand behind Peet. The air was filled with a bittersweet smell that tickled Peet's nose. Hairless, they carried long knives, one for each of their four hands, and they wore jackets lined with metal. They seemed to merge into one another, then separate at will. At the sight of the creatures, one tall and wide, the other short and thin, Peet felt something shift inside of his head.

"Otherworlders," he whispered, a shocked smile on his face.

"Always good in a fight," Maudra said, strapping the axe to her wide back. "And they've a score or two to settle inside the City. But mostly they just want to go back with me, one last time."

"Come, boy," Master Bartolamus said, motioning to Peet. "Join us for my last adventure. We have a gate to un-build."

Peet helped Bartolamus to his feet, and master and apprentice followed the stout woman and the two otherworlders to the mouth of the cave. The old man grabbed something from the table on his way outside. His eyes glowing with a greenish fire, Bartolamus stepped in front of them. He lifted his frail arm, the pieces of a small tower in his hand.

"To the Portal!" Bartolamus cried.

The old man turned and, chanting words in a foreign tongue, cast the pieces of metal down into the valley below. And then he flung himself into the air after them. A burst of greenish-white energy filled the cave, and Peet felt his body lift into the air as well. Bartolamus was—at least for a short time— unbuilding the laws of gravity.

Just before floating out of the cave after his Master, Peet grabbed as many pieces of Bartolamus' Cityscape as he could carry. He had a feeling they would need them for the journey north, and for whatever lay beyond in the mythical City.

With a sudden rush of air, the five companions rose into the air as one and flew like hawks into the north, with the keys to the locked City of All-Worlds—and the Portal at its heart—held tightly in the hands of Bartolamus the Sorcerer.

Bonus Story:
Riverrun Alley

In the ramshackle slum of Riverrun Alley, just east of the City of All-Worlds, winter started early and stayed longer than an uninvited guest, and Tockle the otherworlder was beginning to doubt he'd ever see spring. Perched on the edge of his sleeping mat, he tried to remember a day in his new world without bitter cold and searing wind. But the tall blue being from Quantock was cursed with a painfully short memory, and he couldn't remember what he had eaten last night, much less what life had been like before he entered the Portal that led to Subaridon.

Unfolding his body with a crackling like dead branches breaking, Tockle stepped outside of his hut and checked a wrinkled sheet of well-used paper with his day's tasks scribbled on them. He'd barely finished reading his first chore when one of the two Hagarupk brothers living in the shack next door ran into him.

"Tock!" Grex shouted. "What is doing today?"

"I have work to do on the Old Walls," Tockle said. He shivered and pulled his hood tight over his bald head. "Then I'm meeting a friend at Andros' Bar. If you help me, we can finish early." He gave Grex a weary smile, noticing the way the hairy boy was shaking—either hunger or withdrawal from the drugs he and his brother indulged in. "And lunch will be my treat."

"Deal," Grex said, slapping Tock on the back harder than was needed.

With snow falling around them, Tockle and Grex walked south through the twisting paths of Riverrun Alley, waving and nodding to the other slum dwellers they passed. South of the Zither River and east of the locked and guarded City walls, the Alley was a mish-mash of shacks, boxes, and lean-tos huddled together for warmth. Dirt paths trickled and shifted around the parasitic growths of discarded wood and synthetic brown boards. The only constants were the boundaries of the river and the City walls, and the lights of Andros' Bar on the northern riverbank.

With snow falling around them, they arrived at Tockle's work site after nearly a dozen references to his scribbled directions. For two weeks' worth of food, Tockle had agreed to break pieces of the Old Walls into gravel and haul the gravel the River. He picked up a rock and began smashing. There was always work to do, food money to be earned.

"Max has seller at West Gate," Grex began, watching Tockle work. "Seller put stuff under wagon, Max and buddies hit driver. I grab Blur when driver not looking. Funny stuff, huh?"

"I guess," Tockle said. Through the falling snow, he looked over at Grex's furry smile and had to laugh from his front-mouth. His side-mouths were inhaling deeply, helping him draw strength from the thin air as he laughed. The heat from his exertions had chased away the cold and most of the bad feelings that had been haunting him since the start of winter.

Tockle knew the boys—Max in particular—were addicted to the pulse-tripping temptation of Blur, sold in the cheap southern taverns far from Andros' Bar but close to the City walls. Tockle could imagine the havoc the drug was wreaking on the boys' bodies, making them move four to five times faster than their normal speed, their hearts racing as Blur kicked their nervous systems into overdrive.

"Why do you do it?" he asked Grex. "Take Blur, that is. Isn't there something better you could be doing? Working, maybe, or helping the Guard?"

"Help King's Guard?" Barking laughter, Grex almost fell off the chunk of ruined wall where he sat. "Good joke, Tock. King's Guard help get Grex *killed*."

Tockle slammed the big rock he held in his hands down onto another section of wall, disintegrating it. The gravity of Quantock had been almost five times that of Subaridon. "I'm not joking. Keep using that stuff and it'll kill you."

Grex was silent and unmoving for a long moment, nearly the longest Tockle had seen him that way since they'd met that past summer.

"Why use the Blur? To forget," Grex said at last. "To forget we never fight for *Hagurupk* back home. To forget we stuck here, forever. That why we Blur, Tockle. To forget."

Tockle stopped in mid-swing. He felt a cold wind blow from the north, rushing down at them from the Herders' Hills beyond the slum. Looking up, he saw that the sun was at the top of the sky.

I am supposed to meet someone for lunch, Tockle thought suddenly, fumbling in his vest pocket for his paper. Fertig. Of course.

"Come," he said. "Lunch time."

On their walk back through the Alley to the tavern at the northern edge of Riverrun Alley, as the cold came back to fill his bones with ice, Tockle could still hear Grex's voice, clear in Tockle's unreliable memory: *That why we Blur. To forget.*

In the gray noon light, Tockle and Grex approached a ramshackle building lit from inside by lights of many colors, as if it contained fires of blue, green, orange, and red at every corner. Dangling from the off-kilter front door was a sign reading "Andros' Bar." Below the careful block letters of the tavern's name were messages scratched in three different languages. All three said "All beings welcome. No credit."

"Fertig!" Tock said, knocking his fist on the black wood of the bar in front of a tiny, squid-like being. The glistening, three-foot-tall creature was perched on a box balanced on a bar stool. "It's good to see you again, my friend. You remember Grex, of the Hagurupk?"

A ringlet of eyes turned to Tockle, and then looked Grex up and down. Three of the creature's six tentacles waved in Tockle's direction, and then the creature picked up a shot glass of water and poured it over its oblong head. Fertig the Squibble was in a *mood*.

"Ten minutes late," Fertig squeaked, "and you bring this brute. Last time I saw him, he and his brother were harassing the local traders and avoiding any sort of paying work."

"Fertig," Grex said with a growl. "I growed up, huh?"

"Growed *out* is more like it, from the size of your gut."

"Okay boys," Tockle said, waving at Andros' shadow behind the bar. "Enough bickering. Lunch is on me today. And so are drinks, if you're so inclined."

"Gents," a deep voice said. A blue shadow outlined in glinting white light stood waiting on the other side of the bar.

"Drinks for my friends, Andros," Tockle said, squinting to see the wraith-like tavern owner properly. "I'd like to get three bowls of your best stew as well, along with a loaf of your grainiest bread. And some extra water for the Squibble, if you please." Fertig and Grex ordered their drinks, and Andros slipped away.

Tockle turned to Fertig. "So. What's news?"

Fertig did his best to shrug his non-existent shoulders, his tentacles rippling. "The river might freeze solid if the cold keeps up. Wouldn't be goo—you heard about the wild dogs at this time of year? They're hungrier than us, and twice as mean as any Hagurupk."

Grex waved him off and drank the ale Andros had silently placed in front of him.

"And it's been snowing all week," Tockle said. The feeling of dread mixed with sadness from earlier that morning had returned. "I don't know how people can survive winters here."

"Not much choice," Fertig said, and Grex nodded for the first time in agreement. "Though there's always the celebration us Squibbles have in the River to look forward to, so long as it doesn't freeze up on us. Only five more days."

"Celebration?"

Fertig dumped another shot glass of water over his head. It soaked into his skin before it could reach the box or the barstool below him. "Yeah. We all get together to celebrate the shortest day of the year. At mid-winter. We get drunk, make wild Squibble love, and wrap our tentacles 'round each other until the sun comes up again." He gave a squeaky laugh. "Come on, Ol' Blue. Don't you pay attention to the other races 'round here?"

"I've been living in the City," Tockle said, knowing how hollow his explanation must sound to his friends. "Plus my memory's not..."

"Not hardly there, yeah, I know," Fertig said. "Buy me another drink, will ya, Ol' Blue?"

Tockle snapped four sets of fingers. Ignoring the Squibble's suggestion, he grinned at Grex and turned back to his small, tentacled friend. "So tell me, Fertig. How does this celebration work?"

A nd so, instead of returning to his unfinished job at the Old Walls, Tockle began to learn how others—otherworlders and Subaridon natives alike—survived winters on his new world.

After Fertig had explained the watery parties the Squibble folk would hold in the cold Zither River on the shortest day of the year, Grex reminisced about the indoor battles and feasts held around blazing fires his people would hold at mid-winter on Hagurupk. Excited now about the idea forming in his head, his long fingers snapping constantly, Tockle left Fertig at the bar. He tightened the earrings of translation in both his earlobes. The eroding walls could wait another day. With Grex in tow as his memory, he began talking to the other patrons.

"Winter celebrations?" responded one of the yellow-skinned females at the first table Tockle and Grex visited. "Surely you mean the lightin' ceremony of the Herders. My people would gather at a shepherd's barn and each of us would light a candle. We'd sing songs of shearin' and goodwill 'til the last candle burned out. Every night for a fortnight. Legend had it that at the end of the last night of singin', the winter would be lettin' up at last, and spring not far behind. But that's all in the past now, 'course."

"Singing, candles, cider," muttered Tockle, nodding and sighing from his side-mouths. He glanced at Grex to make sure the hairy boy had caught all the details. "Thank you, miss."

"Ah, you mean the Greentree Times," said a wrinkled grayskin with three eyes at the next table. He flicked his snake-like hair back out of his face and winked at Grex with his sideways fore-eye. "Back on my home world, it happened only once every three years, when the cold would relent long enough for the trees in the middle ring of our caves to blossom. Then we would make prayers to the Good Spirits for the cold to return and drop the leaves of the Greentree to the ground for us as treasure. We'd string the leaves up in our caves to decorate them and remember the kindness of the Spirits. We didn't celebrate the end of the cold, but the opposite. The Wannoshay are at home in the cold, and hate the bright sun's burning rays."

"We held competitions," a long-limbed Walker of Assurinto sitting next to the Wannoshay man said, folding his/her legs up under his/her dark blue cloak. "As soon as the cold forced us indoors, we would challenge one another, man/woman, girl/boychild, elder, to see who was the fastest, the strongest, the most enduring of the Walkers. The Champion was wreathed in the leaves of the agarta tree and given milk from the flying mammals of our forest to drink."

"*Good* ideas," Grex said. He wouldn't stop elbowing Tockle, most likely picturing himself crowned in leaves while his brother slumped over his wine in defeat. "Champions like *Hagurupk*. Very good ideas. I remember these."

A human male with gray-white hair smiled at Tockle's question, and his eyes glazed over as he remembered. "To celebrate winter, we would cut down living trees and set them up inside our house. We dangled pretty strands of silk and hand-made crafts from its boughs, then lit the whole thing up in candles while we waited for gifts wrapped in paper from the Red Elf. As we waited, we would drink concoctions made from frothed eggs and whiskey and sing about flying deer and miracle babies born in stables. Sometimes we would even sing about wanting it to snow more, so we could have a white celebration!"

"Crazy ideas," Grex muttered as they moved away from the table of pink-skinned humans. "The Red Elf!"

"But I like the idea of gifts, Grex." Tockle nodded at the humans before he moved to the table closest to the fire.

"We marked the height of winter," began a massive eight-eyed being encased in a bright silver metal suit, with a glass shield covering his mottled black and brown face, "with a sacrifice. We started the smoking fire on the first day of the Wintermonth, and let it burn until the frosts melted. We ate from the sacrifice for the entire month. We'd usually pick one of our biggest brothers or sisters for the sacrifice. Made for richer eating, of course..."

Tockle gave Grex a wide-eyed look before nodding at the big creature, who was almost taller than he was himself. He stepped back away from the table and the too-hot fire. "Okay, ah...that helps. My thanks to you. We really must be moving on. Grex?"

"We didn't have winter on our planet," a brownish-red female from the world of Nedos said, two tables over. "But we did have the dark months and the bright months, depending on the tilt of the planet and the rays of our twin suns. We paid homage to the gods of light and gathered together every night to share stories of our travels and the magical adventures of our wizard who lived in the frozen land far to the north. Even after we entered the Portal and came to Subaridon, we continued our traditions. But now my people have been scattered, sent to different slums or leaving for one of the outer fort cities. It's hard to pay homage by myself, and nobody around here seems to care about telling stories. Until you two stopped by, that is. What is it you are planning?"

Tockle sat back and chewed his three pairs of lips. His head felt jammed too full of information and stories, and he knew he'd forget most of his facts before he left Andros'.

"I'm not sure," he said. "But I know I like the way your people come together during the harshest time of the winter. Everyone I've talked to seems to do this, in some way, no matter where they are from. I see no reason for that tradition to die out, now that we are exiled from the City and our true homes." Tockle grimaced at the thought and leaned forward. "I daresay we all need a tradition now more than we've ever needed one before."

Tockle dropped off the pile of gravel next to river and turned for another load. The snow continued to fall as Tockle went about his work and the daylight began to fade. He was lost in his planning and the exertions of his task. The emptiness that had made him want to remain in his shack all day, curled up on his mat, had almost entirely faded away. Even the cold air that threatened to freeze shut his side-mouths went unnoticed.

The week passed, colder than ever, and the ground was covered in a foot of dirty snow. Tempers continued to flare, and Andros had to break up a rash of fights in his tavern. Some of the shacks in the southern half of Riverrun Alley had been set on fire, supposedly by members of the King's Guard, looking for trouble—and a missing shipment of Blur—outside the City. And by week's end, for the first time in decades, the Zither River froze solid.

After completing his cleanup of the Old Walls and getting his payment from the members of the Alley's informal council, Tockle bartered half of his two-weeks-worth of food for provisions for his party. As long as the work wasn't too extensive, Grex assisted in the planning, remembering the details of the various traditions for Tockle when Tockle's memory failed him, which was often. Tockle's focus was so much on his new party that he didn't have time to be worried about the packs of wild dogs that were sneaking across the frozen river to attack people and cause almost as much trouble as the King's Guard.

With the help of Grex, who had turned discarded fishing lines into leaf-filled streamers and gathered up all the precious candles he could find from the slum dwellers, Tockle had made so much progress on his celebration that he could scarcely believe it. The once-filthy back room of Andros' bar was filled with painted landscapes of various worlds, strings of leaves, candles, boughs cut from evergreen trees, and all the phosphor lights Tockle could buy for a week's worth of food.

Many of the customers, after eating their lunch in the tavern, stepped into the back room, only to be drawn into the preparations by Tockle. He gave them decorating tasks to do, or taught them one of the five new songs he had created for the mid-winter party planned for the next evening and continuing for a week afterward. Soon the back room was bustling with people, hammering and painting and singing.

Tockle stayed late into the night, putting the final touches on his winter party. All he needed was food and drink, which he would get from Andros tomorrow in exchange for renovating his back room and promising to build a pier onto the river for him after the thaw. Tockle turned off the phosphor lights and closed the door to the back room with a satisfied sigh.

He paused and listened to the soft ticking of the lights mixed in with the soft breath coming from his three mouths. He was the happiest he'd ever been since coming to Riverrun Alley, but there was still something bothering him. Something he had forgotten.

Shrugging, he turned toward his home, humming a song of his own creation from his side-mouth despite the cold. Tomorrow night would be the first night of the new celebration.

* * * * *

During the night, however, visitors came to the party, uninvited and early.

Smoke rose from Andros' Bar when Tockle approached it the next morning. Tockle ran inside and found the back room nearly destroyed. Chairs and tables had been set on fire, and most of the leafy streamers had gone up in flames along with the phosphor lights he had bought. All that kept the whole place from going up was the pressurized sprinkler system Andros had piped into the tavern from the river many years ago, after one fire too many. Only the back room suffered any damage.

Numb, Tockle bent down to pick up the pieces of a broken chair, the same chair he'd stood on yesterday to hang tree boughs from the rafters. He squeezed the bits of wood as if they were weapons.

I won't forget this, he thought. *Not until my dying day—this I'll remember.*

For close to an hour Tockle stood staring at his ruined dream with the broken pieces of the chair in his oversized hands. He felt his head spinning, as if he'd stood up too quickly. The sickening sensation remained with him, growing stronger just like the wind blowing down at him from the north.

Finally, pulling himself away from the wreckage, Tockle stumbled back to his home. He was going to have to break the news to Grex somehow. But before he could raise a hand to enter the brothers' shack, Max came flying backwards out of the door, followed by an enraged Grex.

"Tell!" Grex shouted at his brother. "Tell Tock now!"

Max pulled himself to his feet and raised his head. His face was puffy and covered in dried blood, and he was much thinner than Tockle had remembered him to be.

"Tockle," Max said. "I didn't know they would do that to your place. I just thought it would be fun to go there after having some Blur. I tried to stop them."

Tockle stepped closer, staring numbly at the small silver earrings in each of Max's floppy ears. "Who are you talking about? *Who?*"

"Some of the Guards. The guys we get our stuff from. They came over and saw Andros' place all decked out. They were on Blur, and I didn't have more to give them. They didn't like that. So they trashed the place to teach me and everyone there a lesson. They wanted me to tell you that the King's watching us now. They..."

"Come," Grex said, gripping his brother by the arm with both of his big hands. "Got do cleaning now, *brother.*"

"No." Tockle shook his head, looking at the injuries Max must have suffered from the Guards as well as his brother. His heart ached, and he felt the cold breeze from the north as sharp as ever. "Leave it, boys. I'll help Andros clean it up later. This is my fault." He exhaled through both his side-mouths. "Please. Do not disturb me for the rest of the day."

Before either brother could say anything more, Tockle walked into his shack. Dropping the legs of the ruined chair into the middle of the dirt floor, he began building a fire. He didn't plan on leaving his home for the rest of the day. He had to collect his thoughts and memories before he made one final trip over the wall to track down the people who had ruined his plans. Revenge was his only thought as he covered his head and inhaled smoke in his cold slum home.

A nd so, for the first time since arriving in Subaridon, Tockle underwent a day of remembering. Like a form of confession, the remembrance would cleanse him and guide him, helping him decide what to do next. Wrapped in his blankets, he sat as close to the fire as he could, letting the smoke enter his three mouths and burn away all present-day distractions. The painful memories of his celebration drifted away. For the entire morning his only movement besides inhaling and exhaling was to add another piece of wood to his fire.

By lunchtime he could remember what the City of All-Worlds looked like while he was still living there. The wondrous machines of the Berahite neighborhood, and the many turrets that surrounded the tall King's Tower at the confluence of the Whiting and the Zither rivers. The low buildings of the Research Quarter, connected with walkways and all manners of doors and windows. The red and yellow colors of the Guard, their eyes glaring and him and his fellow otherworlders in the days before the Closure.

When his rumbling stomach told him that the night meal had come and gone, he could remember details about his world Quantock just before he entered the Portal with his five compatriots. The parade that marched them to the building that housed the mythic Portal, and the memory of the singing and music that accompanied them, brought tears to his aching eyes.

And finally, as the fire was burning low and Tockle sipped a bitter tea from the precious leaves he stored on a high shelf of his shack, he remembered his family. Darkness and cold surrounded him in the present, but in his memory he was on the sandy fields of Quantock, sweating under Sectocki, the second sun, and his brothers and sisters were playing next to him. His mother and fathers had stopped by to see him and their other children before they traveled north for the windy season, far from the sand that the children couldn't bear to leave.

Tockle hadn't thought of his family in ages, and tears again threatened. But before his eyes could water, he realized what had been missing all along. What he'd forgotten since coming to this new world.

He'd never had a chance to say goodbye to his family. He and the other soldiers, chosen for their intellect and strength, had been forced to enter the Portal immediately, before anyone could change their minds or the Portal could disappear again. Tockle had been too caught up in the excitement of his new adventure to remember to visit his family again. He'd simply stepped through the Portal and disappeared, never to return.

"Goodbye," he whispered. Gazing into the embers of his fire, smoke in his nose and mouths, he imagined his message being heard over an unimaginable distance.

The slum was covered in silence all around him. Cold air hit his sweaty skin, and he breathed in deeply of the thin, now-familiar mixture of air with all three of his mouths. He smothered the fire with his foot, all thoughts of revenge gone, leaving him only with a grim sense of determination. He stepped out into the cold darkness and headed for Andros' Bar.

W hen Tockle made it back to the tavern, the multi-colored phosphor lights of the main room were dark. Voices echoed from the rear of the empty bar. Tockle's mouths dropped open in shock. He recognized the songs; he had created them only days ago. Despite the smell of smoke still lingering in the air, the singing and talking voices were full of happiness.

Tockle had planned on a long night of cleaning, with occasional breaks to slip over to the bar for drinks with friends. But Andros' tavern area was dark and empty. He hurried through the main room and ducked under the charred doorway leading to the ruined back room.

The multi-colored phosphor lights had been saved from the wreckage, and they lit up the back room. Freshly-hewed tree limbs hung from the shadowy rafters, covering the charred walls, and best of all, Andros had moved his bar and buffet tables into the party area. The ruined chairs and tables had been broken into firewood for the massive bonfire blazing outside, next to the river. Tockle could hear the sound of Fertig the Squibble's voice coming from a hole that had been made in the icy river, accompanied by wild splashing and squeaky laughter.

Dressed in a red suit fringed with mangy gray fur, Grex bounded up to him. His red hat fell onto his eyes as he shouted Tockle's name and launched into a hoarse rendition of the first song Tockle had taught him.

Within an hour, almost all of the people from Riverrun Alley were there. Overcoming his shock and surprise, Tockle found his voice and taught his new songs of winter's end to anyone who would listen. They sang even louder when the wild dogs began to cry outside, and they even forgot about the King's Guard and the warm buildings inside the locked City. Inside Andros' Bar was the only place anyone wanted to be that night.

"What you think, Tock?" Grex shouted.

"It's perfect," he said, accepting a frothy mug from Andros. The taste of Andros' finest brew and the sight of his fellow slum dweller filled Tockle the otherworlder with a warmth he hadn't felt since he'd left home. Tockle was glad, after all this time, that he was finally with family again.

About the Author

Michael Jasper loves to explore the places where the normal meets the strange. In pursuit of this fascination, he has written and published over a dozen novels, three story collections, sixty short stories, and a digital comic with artist Niki Smith.

In the past he attempted bartending, teaching junior high, painting houses, being a secret shopper, working construction, and many more jobs; he prefers fiction writing. For his day job, he works as a technical writer.

He lives with his family in North Carolina, and his website is **michaeljasper.net**.

www.ingramcontent.com/pod-product-compliance
Lightning Source LLC
Chambersburg PA
CBHW020320150626
46552CB00022B/3051